Table of Contents

A few of these stories were previously published in Mizna

A Few Simple Sentences of Introduction

I am not a writer, but when I was young I used to go to a small river by my house and take off my shoes and put my feet in the water. I would tell myself, I have to be a writer. I used to write short stories and poetry, and for a short time I made films. I really wanted to be a writer. But somehow I got involved with politics and couldn't continue writing. But I still carry the love of writing with me.

Writing for me is the act of thought and feeling making love. Just as when a man and woman make love, one out of those millions of his sperm finds her egg and a child is formed. The cells come together slowly, slowly. After nine months the child is born and they give it a name. Writing is making love between thought and feeling.

A lot of times I feel sad. A lot of times, I feel angry or I feel happy—and during many of these times I don't write. But then in one moment, my thoughts and feelings reach each other and my mind becomes pregnant. The ideas grow and grow. They move from this side of my mind to the other side, and after a while I have a story. For me the challenge is to create a new way to tell that story. Sometimes after I finish the story, I bury it in my mind. Once in a while I put it on paper.

The stories you will read come from this experience. Because of my limited English I use a very simple vocabulary. My friend Brian, with whom I share all of my problems, helps me type my stories and correct my grammar. Many thanks to him.

Those stories could happen for many different people in many different parts of the world. I try to not let the particular name of any border limit the sharing of them.

Jean-Luc Godard, the French filmmaker, once said that his movies begin when people leave the theater. I hope my stories begin when you finish reading them. I also believe that if someone is kind enough to give me his or her time to read my work, I should give something in return. A gift of time is so large, and my story is so small in return. Yet I hope with all my heart that these stories are that gift to you.

The House on the Other Side of the Night

I don't remember what day it was when my mother called. It may have been yesterday or the day before. I don't remember the days or years anymore. The only thing I remember are seasons. When I was a child it was different. I knew how many days we had left until the end of the school year. I knew how many hours we had until the weekend. I knew how many minutes we had to wait until the newspaper man came. But now things are changing.

She said, "How are you?"

I said, "I am fine." And I heard the echo down the long-distance line, "I am fine."

"Did you find a job?"

"Yes, Mom."

I am working in the luggage company. My job is to take wooden boxes and cover them with leather and turn them into luggage. Only foreigners around me as I work. My supervisor likes to talk about politics, especially with me. He doesn't like the workers to talk with each other. The job is not too hard, but sometimes I get slivers in my fingers and it takes time to get them out with a needle.

Mom said, "Do you have a good time there?"

"Yes, Mom, I do."

I don't remember which day it was, Friday or Saturday, but I know it was winter time when I went to hide my loneliness in a bottle of beer. I walked into the bar. I ordered a beer. Behind the bartender, on the wall, I saw a map of the place where I was born. And at the bottom of the map the words, "Fuck them."

I complained to the bartender. He called the bouncers. There were three of them and they threw me out the door. I went to another door and tried to talk to the manager, but the bouncers came again. They played basketball with me. I was the basketball. When the police came, I found myself swimming in snow on the parking lot, and later in court, the judge was nice, but his court found me guilty.

Maybe because of this, the next day at the factory I wrote on the outside of one of the boxes, "Nobody chooses the place of their birth."

My mother asked me on the phone, "Why don't you write to me? You are supposed to send me some pictures."

I said, "OK, I will, I will."

When the police came to my mother's house, they confiscated all of our pictures. If we fled to another part of the country, they would use the pictures to identify us.

"But you were supposed to send them years ago."

"Yes, I know Mom, but I promise this time I will."

For a few seconds there was silence on the line, and I knew exactly what my mom was going to ask.

"You're getting old. Don't you want to get married?"

"Who? Me?"

"Yes, you. Haven't you met any nice women?"

"Yes, I have."

She was sitting by the window of the Global Café when I met her. I used to go there because most of the people were foreigners and nobody would make fun of your accent. She was by the window, hiding her long red hair in a black hat.

I walked to her table and asked, "Do you write poetry?"

She said, "Yes, but now I'm writing music. Why?"

I explained that we were going to have a poetry reading for the benefit of our local magazine. My friend Dan believed we needed to find a woman to read because we already had two men.

She said, "Do you write?"

"Yeah."

"Can I see some of your work?"

I gave her a piece to read, a poem that contained these lines:

I take my pen
  Draw two flowers, and a bird, on my wall

  On the loneliness of my flesh
    I draw affection...

A couple of weeks later she came to my place and said she would read. She brought me a drawing—I still have it—of two flowers and a bird.

"For your wall," she said.

I smiled and said, "How about for the loneliness of my flesh?"

She wore a long black dress and carried her cello. She set the cello down and kissed me lightly on the cheek.

I still feel that kiss. Even after I'm dead, I will feel it.

We walked. We walked for days and days. All fall we were walking on beautiful red, orange, and yellow leaves. We talked the whole time.

The poet Rumi once wrote that he carried a lamp through the city, and that the only thing he could see were demons. And he wished only to find a human. That fall, in my head, I began to talk with Rumi and I told him, "I found it, the human you were looking for."

"Yes Mom, I met her."

"Why didn't you marry her?"

Brian said the same thing when we were drinking beer.

I told him, "Because I love her."

Brian said, "That's a good reason to be with her."

"No, that's a good reason *not* to be with her."

Brian said, "I don't understand. Why?"

"Because I don't have anything to give her. In our past, the only thing I could share with her were my problems. I didn't have anything else. I wanted happiness for her. I wish I had something to share with her."

Later, when Brian was drinking hot chocolate and I was drinking coffee he said, "Do you love her?"

"I told you, Brian, I did and I do."

Brian was silent. So I continued.

"But to be in love is worse than to be tortured. When you are tortured, you think about it afterward and you feel proud. You see yourself, a young guy, your hands chained behind your back and two big men are punching you. You make them angry by keeping silent. Do you understand? You are the one in chains, but you are making them angry. Afterward, thinking about it, you feel happy and it makes you strong. But the chains of love are different. To be in love means to be *tortured all the time*, you carry the pain of it all the time. With love you cannot keep silent. You write poems about it, you sing about it, you talk about it."

When I was talking to Brian I used that word *pain*, but now that I think more about it, I don't think it is the right word. Probably the word I should have used is stalwart. To be in love you have to be stalwart all the time. And that's difficult.

Brian said, "What do you mean?"

"You have to be so strong to wish happiness for her all the time."

I don't know if he understood me or not. I hope he did.

My mother said, "What's happened to that nice woman you met?"

"Mom, I don't know."

I went to the Global Café to see her one more time. The name had changed. Hard Times Café. I looked at the seat by the window. All fall I looked in the leaves for her. In the winter I looked in the snow prints. In the spring I asked the birds if they had seen her. If I hadn't lost my hearing in the war, the war that neither my neighbor or I had any part in making, the war that took all his children from him—maybe I could hear her cello when the wind blows from the southwest. In the summer I dreamt of her in a long white dress. I wished her only happiness.

My mother said, "Do you write anything?"

"No. I don't."

"Why not?"

"I can't, because of my mind."

My mind knows how to fly. Once I brought a wounded pigeon to my home. Three or four days later the bird died, but before it did I taught my mind to fly.

Sometimes my mind flies away to sit behind the desk where I sat as a third grader. I wrote my name on that desk. And my mind asks the same questions of the teacher. Or he climbs the fig tree in my front yard. The one from which I fell. Or he plays behind the big tree in the village where I used to play with my cousin in the summer. And he comes back to me, tired, and tells me all these stories and makes me cry. I told him, "My friend says it's not good to cry," and he laughs and says, "Which friend? Do you have any?"

"You didn't tell me what happened to her."

"Mom, love took her away from me."

I heard someone crying. I think it was the neighbor's baby.

I said, "Mom? Mom?" The phone line was dead.

* * *

I wrote that last sentence—"The phone line was dead"—and put my pen down. I looked at the stack of pages in front of me. The title was *Scattered Notes*. I thought: How many times have I sat and written these things down, and each time said, "Okay, this time I'll finish it?"

I picked up the whole stack of paper and put it in the garbage. I left the desk and went to find a book to read. Looking at all my books, I remembered when I went to the bookstore as a child. I was starved for books then. For a long time I would only look at the books through the shop window. The owner finally asked me inside to look at the books. I would stay up late reading them very carefully, opening them just so far so as not to crack the new bindings so they could be sold as new. I always returned them the next morning and got more. I used to need books.

But now I am always tired.

I came back to my desk and picked up a fresh piece of paper for a new story. The blank paper scares me. Maybe the untold stories hide there. I think I should write something, but what?

For years I have wondered why I am so homeless, a nomad, roving. So this story would begin when I was a boy one winter. I picked up my pen and began. I was a boy in bed under many covers and I heard my Mom's voice but tried to act like I was sleeping. I knew what she would ask by the sound of her voice. Buy the bread. Her voice was nicer than normal.

"Get up and buy the bread," she said. Her voice was like warm water. I wanted to slip under the water and go back to sleep. I felt her hand tug the blanket. Cold air rushed across my feet. "Buy the bread, please" she said again, "all the other children are asleep." I lay still with my eyes closed. The warm water flowed over my head, but the cold air now came up my shins. Goosebumps on my legs. "Buy the bread." I pretended to be asleep. "Come now and go buy the bread." The cold was moving up, wrapping around my waist, and I started to shiver, but I kept my eyes closed and didn't move. "You can keep the change."

I threw the blanket off and got dressed and went to the market. On my way I passed the girl's high school. Someone had written graffiti on it the night before. "We need food, not weapons."

I bought the bread, and told the baker what I had seen. He laughed and said, "Are you sure the sign didn't say *bread*?" By the time I returned home, the police were at the wall painting over the sign.

"What's happening?" I asked one of the policemen. "Why are you doing this?"

"Go away," he yelled.

"Why?"

"I said, go away! It's none of your business." He tore off a chunk of my bread and then kicked me in the back.

When I got home I ate then ran to the school, and I saw him and told him about the wall. When everyone had left the classroom for recess and we thought it was safe, we wrote the same thing on the blackboard. We didn't think we'd get caught. We got caught and the teacher took a ruler and beat the palm of each of our hands ten times. Then he made us write 200 times that night "I am stupid."

I put my pen down and stared at the paper. I was taking a shower when he knocked on the door and said he had to leave. I told him, just a minute and I'll come out.

I didn't wash my hair. I just toweled off and got dressed, and walked out of the bathroom.

I hugged him and we said good-bye. Weeks later he was arrested with a few fliers. When they arrested him he tried to kill himself with cyanide. But they forced his mouth open and made him drink dish soap so he would throw up. Later on in prison he tried again by jabbing a needle in his wrist veins over and over, and then tried to jab the needle into his heart, but it was too short. They found him and took him to the hospital.

A few weeks later they executed him. He was 21. When his mother came to claim his body, they made her pay for the bullet that had killed him.

I should write about him someday, but who would believe it?

I left my desk and went to the bathroom to get a needle. The slivers in my fingers hurt. These I'd gotten from making a piece of black luggage that looked identical to the luggage I carried across the border.

I walk into my bedroom and lie down on the bed. I finish my cigarette and stub it out in the ashtray and watch the shadows on the wall lengthen as the sun sets. My mother watches the sun rise on her home. The sun will climb out of the sea as if washed clean. The fishermen will return from the sea and she will buy their catch in the market. The small tables are close to each other and everyone is yelling, "Fresh fish! Shrimp!"

She walks home with a couple sole. On her way she stops at the bakery to buy bread. At home she drinks tea. The house is empty and the only sound she hears is of the ocean waves. She goes out into the garden. Roses and nasturtiums line the path to where she grows herbs. She walks a few steps, stops, and bends to a rose to smell it.

At the herbs, she kneels and pulls a few weeds then picks sweet basil leaves. As she works she sings a song to herself, the song she sang while nursing my younger sister and probably me. Her mother sang it to her just as her grandmother had sung it to her mother. She sings and is unaware even that she is singing. No one knows who wrote it, but it is lovely and sad.

Behind me lies the farm
Ahead lies Yellow Mountain.
The moon flies above the lake

I can see my love swimming.
I wish I had a golden sun
to give your father,
to buy you.

She leaves the garden singing, goes to the kitchen
and washes the basil. Then she cleans the fish
and cooks them with garlic and curry and the
smell fills the entire house. But she does not eat.
She packs the fish into a lunch.

My mother rides the bus down the dirt road to
my father's grave. The graveyard is much bigger
than it used to be. So many young people now.
Near my father, three of his nephews. She sits at
the grave and wishes her children could be there
to share the food. She complains to my father
about the children, they don't listen. He keeps
silent. In the past, it was, he would complain
while she kept silent. Things are changing.

She rides the bus back home. At the end of the
day she sits on the couch near the window where
she can see the garden. She sews the image of a
rose into some fabric. She sews until night begins
to run into the day and the sun sets on her home.
She can see the evening star. She puts her sewing
down, gazes at the empty frame on the wall and
imagines the face of her children.

The sun starts to climb from behind the tall buildings to reach my apartment window. I see my mother's shadow on the wall. I put my cigarette into the ashtray. The ashtray is full now. I think I should write about these things someday.

The alarm clock rings the alarm clock of paying rent. I have to go. Wooden boxes are calling me.

Overture

I asked that prostitute
   Is not life a beach?
she responded:
   have three children.
   have not paid the rent.
I asked the bird
   How much rent do you pay for the tree?

I take my pen
   Draw two flowers, and a bird, on my wall.
   On the loneliness of my flesh
   I draw affection.
   I draw a glass of milk for our neighbor's
children
   ...a smile on my face.

I draw a house...
   for the homeless man
      who sleeps in the bus stop

In the night sky I draw the sun.

I take my eraser
and erase hate from my mind
   erase the streets from walking girls
   erase the word war from all languages
   all nation borders
   I erase the geographical map

I multiply peace by number of mass's heartbeats
with "division" I divide wealth
I subtract poverty from books

I invite fishes from the lakes to the
  party in the ocean

Follow the Rain

John threw open the back door and tossed his backpack under the bench with his shoes. Unzipping the pack's rear pocket, he took out the thin black computer disk he had carried there for three days, three whole days. It had felt like a week. He took the stairs to the family library two at a time.

The library was small but well stocked. Most of the books went unread, pulled from their shelves only to be dusted every month. This was John's favorite time of day, when only he and his mother were at home, and he had the library and its computer all to himself.

Reaching behind the computer, he flipped the switch on and while it clicked and whirred into life, he inserted the floppy disk into the slot. The computer paused a moment before beginning a new series of ticking sounds confirming that it was reading the disk.

While he waited, John reached for a glass beside the computer. It was empty. He was thirsty and considered calling his mother to fill it, but just then the screen brightened with a field of blue. He forgot his thirst.

The computer game was a gift for his eleventh
birthday, three days earlier. Twenty-five levels.
The first day he got to level two. Yesterday, level
three. He had played until eight o'clock when his
favorite TV show came on, and then he had
returned the disk to his backpack. John had
carried it there all day, anticipating this time,
when he might be able to hit level five.

Along the right side of the screen a menu
appeared. He clicked "BUILD" and the screen
filled with a landscape, hilly and green, and
dotted with farms and villages. Next he clicked
on "WEAPONS" and began choosing an array of
armaments: cannons, jet fighters, tanks, bombers,
even the exact kinds of bombs the planes
carried—ship-to-shore, air-to-air, surface-to-air.
Everything. Drawing all of his weapons into one
corner of the screen, he built his base and added
twenty soldiers to it.

"START." John drew a square around five soldiers
and two tanks, then clicked on a group of houses
in the far-off village. The soldiers and tank
advanced on the house and as they did, figures
appeared from inside it. Instantly the tank and
soldiers opened fire. Streaks of red permeated
the house, exploding the roof and shattering the
windows. The figures were mown down, then
they simply disappeared.

Further up the screen a soldier popped up from behind a hill and fired back at John. He drew another square around a jet fighter and sent it after the soldier. The fighter climbed into the electric blue sky and John clicked on "air-to-surface." A streak of hot orange sped from the plane to the hill.

Direct hit. The screen filled with smoke, then went blank for a second. At that moment John looked at the empty glass on the desk and remembered his thirst.

"Mother, I'm thirsty!"

Ali lay down on his belly and spread his arms out. The soil near the little spring was rocky. Winter had been long and harsh and the rocks were still cold under his fingers. He put his face down into the water and sucked it. It was so cold his teeth hurt and he stopped for a moment. Then he drank again until his thirst was gone. Beside him lay a goatskin bag and, dunking it into the water, he filled it.

Again he bent his face to the water, this time to wash it, but stopped. Others might want this water to drink. He stood and walked a few steps to his left. There the spring bubbled over and filled a small pool below. He knelt and washed, then picked up the goatskin and placed it on his shoulder.

His home wasn't far, just 400 yards, but as he
walked he remembered this same trip last year
and the year before, when the goatskin had felt so
heavy on his shoulder. Last year he had to stop to
catch his breath, once at the top of the hill near
the spring, and again near his house. This time
the bag was easy to carry. He was growing up.

Last year had been so dry. This year Ali hoped for
a wet spring. But even if the rains did come, the
village would still not have water. Father said it
was the war. People cannot build a water system
in the middle of a war. Ever since Ali could
remember there had been a war. As he walked he
kicked up the dust.

Perhaps his father's crops would grow well this
year. If they grew tall and rich, Ali would get his
wish—the movie. Last year his father had
promised him that if the crops were good he
could see the movie. The funny movie in the city.
His friend Mohammed had seen it and talked of it
month after month. Ali wanted to see the movie
this year.

A fig tree stood just outside Ali's house. His
father had planted it eleven years prior, at Ali's
birth. Kneeling at the base of his tree, Ali opened
the goatskin and poured the water slowly around
its roots. Again he hoped for rain.

Ali returned to the spring to fill the goatskin.
This time he walked to his house and upon
entering, set the goatskin in a corner of the room.
His mother looked at him.

Mother said, "Do you want Coke or orange juice?"

John said, "Coke, please."

John was frustrated with the game. After several
tries he could get no further than level four.
Mother walked into the room with a glass of
Coke.

She said, "You should do your homework."

He looked at his watch and snapped off the
computer. He went to his own room and turned
on the TV. Movie time.

It was getting dark. Ali lit the gas lamp in the
room. He began his homework, unaware of any
sense of time. He simply did it until it was done
and when he was tired, he unrolled his mattress
in the corner of the room and went to sleep.

John woke up to the sound of the TV that he'd
left on all night long. He brushed his teeth, took
a shower, and got dressed before going
downstairs to look for breakfast. In the kitchen
cupboard lay the bread—five different kinds—

whole wheat, cinnamon, sourdough, English muffins, bagels.

John said, "Mom, what should I eat? There's nothing to eat. No white bread."

Mother said, "You should eat something."

Ali picked up the bread. It was a little dry. He dipped his fingers into a bowl of water and sprinkled it on the bread. He thought of asking his mother for eggs, but he knew she wanted to trade the eggs for sugar, and he felt embarrassed. He picked up an onion from the basket hanging on the wall and set it on the floor. Hitting it once with his fist, he broke open the onion. Ali picked up the white pieces, salted them, and put them on his bread. Taking his first bite, he picked up his book and walked out of the house.

On the way to school, Ali looked at the sky and asked Mohammed, "Do you think it will rain?"

Mohammed said, "I hope so."
John said, "Shit, it looks like it's going to rain today! Why today? It'll ruin our basketball game."

Troy said, "If it rains, what are you going to do?"

John said, "I think I'll go home and rent a video and eat a pizza."

They walked into the classroom and took their seats. High on the wall was a TV set. It was off. John put his books away, reached down to his wristwatch and pressed a button. The TV came on. A talk show from New York. The teacher looked quickly up at the set. John touched another button on his watch to shut it off. The teacher looked mad. John turned it back on. Then off again.

The teacher said, "Quiet please. You are supposed to choose your subject and write your essay."

Ali sat close to the table. The string could only reach so far. One end of the string was tied to his shirt button, the other to his pencil. Last week he'd lost his pencil and, without it, school had been hard. It took two days to get another and he had no intention of losing this one. But with the new one tied to his shirt, he had to stay close to the table and make it reach.

He began to write, "Follow the rain."

Mohammed looked at Ali's paper. Ali turned his notebook so Mohammed could not see and he looked out the window.

Rain began to fall on the window.

"Look, it's raining," John said. "Guess I'm going to go home and rent a movie and order a pizza. We can play basketball tomorrow."

Just then the school bell rang. John and Troy stood up to go. Troy asked, "What subject did you choose?"

John said, "Pizza. That was what I was thinking about. "He laughed and asked Troy, "What subject did you choose?"

Troy said, "War."

Ali said, "War?"
Mohammed said, "Yes, war."

Ali said, "Why war? Do you know why they are fighting? "

Yes, for God," said Mohammed.

"For God?"

Mohammed said, "Yeah, my father said that. Why did you choose the rain?"

"Because it's important for us," Ali said.

"Everyone knows that," Mohammed said.

Ali said, "Not everybody. Last year when my mother was sick, we took our cow to the market and we saw a man who said he did not like the rain because his shoes got dirty."

Mohammed didn't say anything more.

They left the school and walked to the road leading to their village. The sky was cloudy but held no rain. Ali looked at the sky. The clouds were thick and heavy and seemed to lay on this heart.

As they approached their village, Ali and Mohammed met people on the road carrying packages. They were leaving because the war was drawing closer now.

Mohammed said, "Are you going to move?"

Ali said, "Where could we go? We don't want to live in the camp. How about you?"

Mohammed said, "No, I don't think so."

Mohammed talked about the movie until they got home. Ali opened his door.

John stepped into his house with a video in one hand a pizza box in the other. Troy had to go home early, so John watched the movie and ate the entire pizza himself.

The next day his stomach hurt and he stayed home all day from school. He spent the day in the library, quietly playing the computer game. He clicked on a small brick building, then called up several jet fighters to attack. The fighters raced across the electronic landscape and emptied several bombs on the building.

Ali woke but couldn't see anything. The smoke was thick and there were no lights on. He felt a sharp pain in his left leg from the knee down. The heavy table had saved him, but shrapnel had ripped into his leg and it was bleeding badly. He could hear the sound of sawing as if someone was cutting down a tree. He opened his eyes and saw his mother.

Mother said, "Why are you screaming?"

John said, "I just finished this level."

Mother said, "Do you feel better?"

Ali said, "Yes. Thanks."

One week passed for Ali in the hospital.
Sometimes he felt a funny itching feeling in his
left foot, but when he reached down to scratch it,
there was only air. Everything below his knee was
gone.

At noon on the eighth day, Father came to the
hospital. He brought crutches with him, made of
new wood. The wood smelled familiar to Ali.
Father looked at him.

Father said, "We're going to Hawaii for a week."

John had a good time playing in the Hawaiian
surf and sand, though he had a painful sunburn
for the first two days. But the week went by so
fast, and it was time to return home before he
knew it.

Ali rode in the back of the small truck on his way
home from the hospital. He was lying down, but
as the truck approached the city he struggled to
sit up. He looked over the truck railing as it was
passing the movie theater. Ali strained to see
what was playing at the theater.

When the truck arrived at the house, Ali looked
for his tree, but all he found was empty space.
High up on the hills, on Mohammed's house, he
saw a black flag flying.

Two months passed and John reached level twenty-five. He got bored by then, and got a new game.

The land got used to the new wheat, the wheat got used to the wind, and Ali learned how to walk well with his crutches. He walked outside the village in the fields. The wheat brushed the raw end of his half leg. He saw his mother coming from far away. She looked much older now. Watching her carry the water made him sad. He slumped on his crutches, making them look taller, as if they were a growing tree in the spring.

Ali looked at the sky, it was cloudy. Tears came to his eyes. His mother approached and he put his head down, and a few raindrops fell to the thirsty soil. Mother looked at him.

Mother said, "Do you want popcorn, too?"

John said, "Yes."

Mother bought the jumbo size and they walked into the theater. John sat down and put the popcorn between his legs. He held the drink in his right hand. The movie started.

Story for Sale

We walked a long time together until we came to the wall. It was in the middle of the city and painted with brilliant yellow lilies. There we stopped and he laid the day's newspaper out on the sidewalk. On top of that he stacked pages of writing paper, each page filled with his neat flowing hand in black ink. For a while he sat and read the pages. Then he stood upright and called, "Story for sale! Story for sale!"

From time to time he would stop and bend down to pick up a page and read it. It was in his own language and he read it out loud to anyone who had passed.

"What are you doing?" I asked him.

He looked up at me and said, "I'm trying to sell these stories." And he picked up one of them and showed it to me.

"See, I wrote this story about the time you and I were in the demonstration and we carried the placards that said, 'freedom or death.' Remember? The soldiers shot at us and our friend was wounded. Remember? We took him to the hospital but he died anyway. His blood was all over our clothes. Instead of washing them, we took them off and buried them in the garden. We thought beautiful red flowers would spring from that ground. Remember?"

"The same place we buried the books when we wanted to leave," he said. "Do you remember? You planted Balzac's 'The Lily of the Valley' and said when we come back it will grow. Do you think it's growing now?"

I kept silent and tried to imagine the garden full of lilies and red flowers. He tried to break the silence by picking up more pages.

"How about this one? This was about the time we were young and we were trying to make that documentary. The day we got arrested and they broke the camera and threw us in jail and beat us up. You cried."

"No, I didn't," I said.

"You cried."

"No, I didn't."

"You *cried*."

I said, "They beat us up. We didn't do anything wrong. All we wanted to do was make a little movie. To show the real life of the people."

"But you cried," he said.

"I couldn't sleep. My whole body hurt. The concrete they threw us on was freezing, and any place I moved hurt. And remember the guard hit my right eye with his military boot."

"But you cried."

"OK, I did, but it was night, and I didn't let them see it. I didn't cry in front of them."

"You cried."

I put my head down at this point and said nothing. He turned and called out again, "Story for sale! Story for sale! For a cup of coffee. Just for a cup of coffee." After several minutes he turned back to me and asked, "Why is no one interested in these stories?"

"Nobody can read this language."

"But the language isn't important. The important thing is the feeling. Sometimes you can read a thing but still not feel it."

"But all these things," I pointed to the pages at his feet, "They're all about your life. You should write about something different."

He gazed for a few seconds at the newspaper underneath his pages. Then he looked up and screamed, "Story for sale! Please tell me you will buy it! Then I will start it the way you want it. I'll write about what you want. I will finish it the way you want. Story for sale!"

At that moment a light rain began falling.

"Let's go," I said. "It's raining now. We'll get cold here."

He looked down at the pages at his feet. "Look," he said, "the ink is starting to run. The words are running. See, that story about Ali? I remember the day I wrote it, I couldn't finish it. Ali had his leg blown off by a bomb and he walked with a crutch his father made from a tree in their family yard. I did not want to finish Ali's story that way. But look, now his leg is growing back, like wheat in the spring. He is running to his mother. Now he can help her carry water."

"Stop. Let them run," I said. "We should go."

"Why?"

I know he wants to argue, just as he did when we were young. He likes to do that. I remember the time when we questioned everything. But daily

life is so hard now. Our hair is gray. I have no
energy for that now. I don't want to give him a
chance.

"Let's go," I said again. "Please. Here, I've got my
umbrella." I started to pop it open.

He said, "No. Close it. Rain is life. Why run
away from it?" And he picked up another poem
to read.

We grew up together. We spent all our lives
together. I know him very well. I picked up all
the pages at his feet, and started to read the same
lines with him. We walked home together.

He jumped into my bed and said, "You cried that
night."

I lay down in the bed, but couldn't sleep. My
whole body hurt, the same as that night on the
concrete. I put my finger in the slim little scar
above my right eye. Years have passed but I still
wonder, why did I cry that night? I remember the
morning after—how more than anything I
wanted to take a shower and wash the tears off
my face so they could never see them.

Then the sun was slowly walking into my room,
pulling the covers back off the bed.

I got in the shower. The drops of water fell on me
as the rain had done last night. I felt alive. I let
the shower run—I liked the sound of it—and
stood in front of the mirror. It was covered with
steam and I wiped it with my towel.

He was in front of me. His hair was messed like
mine. I picked up the brush and combed his hair.
He smiled.

Chapter Seven

The winds come and pass through the farm and the cornfields start to dance. It goes through the windows, passing by the old man near the window and reaches the young woman sitting on the couch. She moves her hair away from her face and hangs up the phone, picks up her purse, looks inside for car keys. Finding the keys she walks out of the house; gets into the car, and turns it on.

She pauses: turns the car off; walks into the house, and goes straight upstairs; yelling at the writer. "I don't like this story anymore. I don't want to be a character in this story. It's boring. I don't like this guy, I am not going to see him."

The writer puts down his coffee cup and looks at the page in front of him. "What's going on? You're supposed to get in the car and drive away. Mike is waiting for you." He picks up his pen to add, "and drove away." She pulls the last page out from under his pen and tears it into pieces. "It looks like you don't understand. I don't like this guy, I don't want to go there." The writer moves back in the chair and picks up a cigarette, lights it and inhales deeply. Exhaling the smoke he looks at the woman and says, "Just tell me why you don't want to see Mike?" She pulls out a chair and slides it closer to the table, sits down, and puts her purse on the table and says, "I don't want to go there." The writer gazes at her and asks why. She keeps her head down and twirls with her hair. "The only thing he wants to do is take me to the woods to talk to the birds and he thinks he can speak their language." The writer blows smoke in the air and asks, " and what's wrong with that?" The woman says, " look, its a beautiful day, I want to do something exciting."

The writer is silent. He goes back through the last few pages and re-reads them. He puts them down and says, "Do you want to see that bartender again?" The woman doesn't say anything. "You had fun with him," the writer said, "you thought he was gorgeous. You remember the first night you met him, you stayed until the bar closed and then went to his house, made love all night. You made breakfast together the next morning and then went running. The next week you drove all the way just to pick him up and bring him to town. You rented that motel room and made love to him. You told all of your friends you loved him." He looked in her eyes and said, "What do you think? Do you want to go out with him again?"

The woman gazes at her hands with her head down. She looks up and says, "But he is violent. He told me that he thinks he killed someone.

Five people attacked him and he took a knife and stabbed one of them and he thinks he killed him." The writer says, "yes I had to put that stuff in the story. ...You see, people like that sort of stuff ....I mean sex, violence, and nature. I have to write something that sells."

The woman leaves the chair and walks across the room. She pauses...and in a soft voice says, "I have to be honest with you. I love someone else." The writer jumps up from his chair. "What?" Her soft voice continues, "I love someone else." The writer finishes his cigarette, puts it out in the ashtray and picks up another, lights it and says, "You like someone else don't you? "Who's the guy?"

The woman looks back at the writer. Pauses and says "John on page 33". Quickly the writer finds page 33 and reads it and says "John!!! You are only supposed to help him fill out an application" " see ...you left me with him to get coffee....we had a long conversation . He told me that his company laid off its workers relocated to Mexico for cheaper labor. And for the next 20 pages I was thinking about him....and for your information for the last fifteen pages while I was lying in bed with Mike I was thinking about John. I can't stop thinking about John, I love him."

The writer picks up his pen and jots a few notes, and asks, "Did he lose his job? The woman nods her head. "That's good. In the next chapter I will set you up with him and you can go out with him and you guys can talk about politics. People will love it." The woman says, "How about now, how about in this chapter?" The writer says, "Just for a few more pages, go out with Mike, then it will be over." Excitedly, the woman asks, "But how?" With an equally excited voice the writer answers, "That's easy. You're going to cheat on him and he will find out and you guys will have a big fight and it will be over. You can see John. I promise."

The woman stands up and takes a cigarette from the writer's pack and asks, "Who is that old man I live with? Why don't we talk?" The writer starts moving his hand again and says, "That's your father. You guys are from two different generations. You don't have anything in common. He's worried about the farm. He's never seen it so dry." The woman asks, "One more thing, who is that guy who calls me and I have to tell him I'm busy, that I have company?" The writer says, "That's your ex-boyfriend. This is the mystery in the story. At the end of the book you will receive a letter from him, and when you try to contact him you will find out he is dead. He will write the letter just a day before he dies. And that is the tragedy. It will look like a soap opera. You see...people like this sort of stuff." The woman says, "But I can't handle it, he has a strange voice and it makes me nervous." The writer says, "But what can I do about it?" The woman comes back and sits in the chair and says, "Simple. Stop him from calling me. I don't mind if I receive a letter. But I don't like hearing that strange voice anymore."

The writer picks up his glasses, cleans them off and puts them on his head and says, "We will talk about it in the next chapter". He picks up a fresh piece of paper and starts to write:

 The winds come and pass through the farm and the cornfields start to dance. It goes through the windows, passing by the old man near the window and reaches the young woman sitting on the couch. She moves her hair away from her face and hangs up the phone, picks up her purse, looks inside for car keys. Finding the keys she walks out of the house; gets into the car, and turns it on and drive away.

Spring Comes Through the South Window

They began to play with each other, the earth under the sun. The earth breathed louder and faster, getting warmer and warmer as if they made love.

The man closed the north window and looked at his wife and said, "It looks like the war is getting closer. I can smell the smoke from the guns."

The woman opened the other window and looked out at the garden and she smelled the daffodils. "But spring is here. Come, dear."

The man walked to her at the window and put his arm around her and they breathed together. The garden was filled with fresh mint, little carrots, basil and parsley, daffodils, and tiny pink roses.

The man said, "The garden is pregnant, like you." He touched her stomach. "Do you think today is the day? It was supposed to be yesterday."

"I don't know. God knows," she said.

He knelt down beside her there at the window and put his ear against her stomach. The smell of the daffodils and the sounds of the baby's heartbeat filled him.

He left her there to go buy the spring gifts, things to celebrate the baby's arrival. A little candy and some fruit—if he could find them. As he walked out the door she called to him, "Please water the garden before you go."

He watered the plants and, going out the garden door, waved to her still in the window.

He passed the school. It made him sorry to look at it now. A pile of rubble. On the first day of the air war, the planes had come out and ruined it. He could see himself inside the school years ago playing with his friends. He kept walking. He heard a small plane high in the sky.

All the way to the shops, he thought they should leave. The war coming so close now. He and his wife argued about it before. But they were both born there. Their baby should be born there, too.

He arrived at the shop with the vegetables on a table outside. He stepped inside and said hello to the owner. Behind the owner were shelves of vegetables and a scale.

The shop owner asked about the baby. "No, not yet. Maybe today or tomorrow."

The shop owner said: "What do you want here? You should be at home with her."

"I know, but I promised her last night that I would go and buy some things to celebrate spring. She wanted me to."

There weren't many things left in the shop. The war was on. But he picked up a few oranges, a couple of boxes of cookies, a few cans of tuna.

"No fresh fish now. The sea is occupied with battleships. So we'll celebrate with a can."

The shop owner said, "You're lucky that we still have it in a can." He put rice in a bag.

The man came and put his goods on the counter. The shop owner totaled them up and the man gave the shop owner his money, said good-bye, and left. The shop owner said: "Take care of your wife. Hopefully next year we'll have fresh fish."

He walked out of the shop and the shop owner kept cleaning the counter and turned on the radio. Nothing much on the radio. He turned it off and sat down behind the counter. The next customer walked in. An older man asked if he had dry milk.

The owner looked at him and said: "You're too old to drink dry milk!"

They both laughed and the old man said, "I know, but I want it for my neighbor's baby."

"Why is that? What's wrong with the baby's father? Send you all the way over for it!"

"He lost his dad in the air attack. Now he and his mother live with us and they take care of me and my wife."

"How old is the baby?"

"Only three months."

"I'm sorry, I don't have any. But wait, maybe I can do something for you."

He went to the back of the shop, the room that was a part of his own house, and he got a bag of dried milk. This was for his own grandson. He gave it to the old man. The old man wanted to pay him for it.

"No, no. No money. This is a gift. Let me have some of the pleasure of helping to take care of the little boy."

"Thank you," the old man said, and walked out of the shop. He closed the door and walked down the street. He hoped to find a taxi, otherwise it would be a long walk. God must have heard him: he turned the corner and there was a taxi. He got in.

"Hello, father," the driver said. "Where are you going?"

"To Rose Boulevard."

"That's a long way from here to there. How did you get here?"

"I don't know. I just kept walking from street to street, shop to shop, to find this." And he held up the bag of dried milk.

They drove together and the driver adjusted the mirror so he could see the old man's face.

The old man said, "Why are you here? You didn't leave?"

"No. Where should I go? People need a taxi. Anyway, if I wanted to leave, who would give you a ride? Sometimes I'm a taxi driver, sometimes I'm an ambulance driver, sometimes I help people move. It's an ugly war. We are human beings, we should help each other, not kill each other."

He looked back in the mirror again at the old man and said, "Who do you think will win this war?"

The old man had his glasses on and was trying to read the label on the milk. "Those who make the arms," he answered.

The taxi driver didn't know what to say. He went into deep thought.

They arrived at Rose Boulevard and at the first light turned right to street number two. The man got out and handed his money to the driver. The driver, though, was still in deep thought. He turned back to the city. A few blocks away, he saw a solider walking. He stopped in front of him.

"Where are you going?" he asked.

"To the military camp, the one by the rail station."

"Get in, I'll give you a ride."

"Oh, no thank you. I don't have money."

"I didn't ask you if you had money or not, I just said get in. I'm going that way anyway."

The soldier got in and asked the driver, "Why are you going that way?"

"I bought some groceries for home and I want to drop them off so my wife can cook them for our spring celebration."

"The driver asked the soldier, "Where have you been?"

"At the public bath. For the last three months I've had to wash myself with cold water. I haven't had a bath in three months. I've come from the front lines."

The taxi driver asked him, "Do you know who will win this war?"

The soldier looked at him. "No."

"Let me tell you. The ones who make the arms."

The soldier started to laugh. "That's not us. And neither is it them."

He dropped the soldier off at the base. The soldier walked inside the camp and saw his friend driving a jeep. Abram, the driver, asked him, "Are you coming along?"

"No," he said. "I'll sleep here tonight. Tomorrow
I'll be there."
Abram said, "OK, take care, I'll see you
tomorrow." He drove away.

He drove to the front lines and began singing a
song to himself. It was a spring song he'd known
since he was a child.

It's raining, it's raining,
the ground is getting wet
My dear love, do not worry,
Everything is getting better.
Winter is going, Spring is coming soon.

When he got to the front lines he saw his friend
Mohammed. He called him. "Hey, Mo! Where
are you going?"

Mo called back, "I have guard duty. I'll be back
tonight to see you."

Mo kept walking. A year ago today was his
sister's wedding. How they'd danced that night.
The men had taken long wooden poles and held
them in both hands high over their heads and
danced all night. As he walked he raised his rifle
over his head, just like that night, and began to
dance as we walked. He looked like he was
drunk. Drunk with the smells of spring and his

own memory. He saw the wedding in front of him, all his friends, all his family, and he danced.

There was a flash of light, and he found himself on the ground looking up at the sky. He didn't know for how long he lay there, but he heard someone talking to him in the enemy's language. He turned toward the sound. Yes, it was the enemy.

The enemy was bandaging him. His leg. His chest. Now the enemy was picking him up and carrying him. The enemy didn't carry him away to the front line, but away from it, back toward his own friends. The enemy sat him down on the thick grass and leaned him up against a boulder. They looked at each other for just a moment—the enemy's face was kind—then the enemy laid his canteen next to Mohammed. The enemy stood and left, but that picture of kindness pressed itself into Mohammed's eye and heart.

He closed his eyes for just a moment but a bright light pulled them open again. The doctor was saying, "Can you hear me?" and squeezing his hand.

He closed his eyes again and pushed back against the doctor's hand. The doctor pulled his hand away and told the nurse, "He stepped on a mine, but he was lucky. Someone bandaged him. They knew what they were doing. Now, this is all I can do."

The doctor ran to the delivery ward to check the baby.

He said to the woman, "I'm sorry I couldn't be here when the baby arrived. It looks like the nurse was able to help you, though."

He checked the baby boy and said, "Perfect." He handed the child to the mother.
She grabbed the little boy and kissed him.

The woman passed the baby to her husband. He looked down at him and kissed the baby too. The baby began to cry and the man handed him back to his wife to nurse.

"You should go," she said. "It's getting late. Please go home and have a good sleep. We will have a whole life with this child."

He came to her and kissed her, then the baby. He turned to go. At the door he stopped and looked back at her.

She smiled at him and said, "You can come back tomorrow morning. Don't forget, though—water the garden."

Behind The Wall

The café was full when she turned from the register. She scanned the small room: the few tables were filled with couples, a group of college kids smoking, a few old men. In the corner, under the television and its flashing MTV images, sat a man. He was alone but his was the only table with a spare chair. He had dark eyes and skin and black hair graying at the temples. He was writing on a napkin. She glanced at other tables. There wasn't an open chair anywhere.

"Can we share the table?"

He looked up for only a second. His eyes were sad. "Yes, please," and he gestured with his hand. Returning to his writing, he said quietly, "We should share life. The table is nothing."

"What?"

He gestured again at the chair then waved his hand in the air. "Nothing. Please have a seat."

She poured cream into her coffee and pulled a pack of cigarettes from her purse. She lit one and blew the smoke politely over his head.

"What are you writing?"

He finished a line and looked at it before answering. "A poem."

"What kind of poem?"

"Here"

He slid the napkin across the table. The handwriting was small and neat and florid, even as it coursed across the cheap, wrinkled napkin.

> *It is snowing.*
> *No one to talk to.*
> *No one to walk to.*
> *No window waits for me.*
> *No door opens for me.*
> *I hear my name*
> *from far,*
> *far*
> *away.*
> *Denna is calling me.*
> *I pick up some snow*
> *and throw it*
> *to my memory.*

She tossed the napkin across the table.

"Who is Denna?"

"It's the name of a mountain."

She didn't know what to say next. She chose the polite thing.

"How tall is it?"

"I don't know exactly. It used to be a volcano, but now it's dormant and has a lake in its top."

He looked out the window to the busy street.
The buses, the students, the other shop windows.
The whole scene covered with new snow.

"It's a beautiful day," he said.

The woman gave him a strange look. "But it's snowing."

"That makes it more beautiful."

She picked up her cigarette and looked at the TV and tried to ignore him.

"Who is that singer, that man?" he asked.

"You don't know?"

"No."

"You really don't know?"

"No, I don't."

She kindly told him it was Johnny Cash.

Just then, the girl at the counter called his order. "Number nine." He went to pick up his sandwich, and as he reached for it the girl behind the counter repeated, quietly, "Number nine."

"Put him in number nine." They had grabbed him by both arms and thrown him into cell nine. "Now you can write all the poetry you want," they'd said and laughed. The walls, the ceiling, the floor, everything was concrete. After several days he had stepped off the cell's dimensions: ten down its length, five across. A single bulb behind a metal cage in the ceiling. A heavy steel door with a small barred window that only the guards could open from the outside. No windows. The walls were thick and he could hear and see no one else.

He sat at the table. The sandwich was cut in half. He took one half and held the plate out for her.

"Would you like some?"

She raised her eyebrows and scowled. Three little syllables, each said with an emphasis. "No. Thank. You."

She stabbed her cigarette out and nervously ripped another from the pack and lit it. She looked out the window like she was trapped. She drummed her fingers on the table.

It was the same sound as from cell ten. The first time he heard it, it was a surprise and he didn't know from where it came. He listened hard. Then he stood and put his ear to each cold wall in the cell and finally found the tapping just over the head of his bed.

He took the metal cup and tapped back. A pause, then the same taps. He heard a muffled voice. "Use the cup to listen." He put the cup to his ear.

"What is your crime?" a man's voice said.

"I don't know. They came and took me from high school. I published a poem."

"Can you read it for me?"

He didn't know what to do. He was scared. Who was behind the wall? Police? Why did he want him to read? What would happen? Then he thought, what the hell. Life couldn't get much worse. It was a strange moment: he put his mouth to the cold concrete and spoke his poem.

"Say it again," he heard through the wall. "The last lines."

Perhaps silence may be broken
Perhaps winter may leave.
Perhaps there is hope.
Perhaps the land is pregnant.
Perhaps there is spring
A tomorrow.

Someone said:
Forward?

He heard laughter through the wall and pressed his ear against the cup.

"That's the reason you're here. It's too strong. How old are you?"

"In September, I'll be sixteen."

"Don't worry," the man said, "you'll graduate from *this* university. We have a lot to learn from each other."

The boy didn't understand what he meant. Later on he found out the man in cell ten was a philosophy professor from the university. His crime was translating and publishing a book. That was seven years ago. Six months ago they threw him back in cell ten for trying to organize a prison strike.

Every morning the boy would wake up to the sound from cell ten. "It is a beautiful day. Open the window of your heart. You'll see."

He looked down at his hands. They were busy pulling bits of bread apart, rolling and shaping them into odd little pieces. He didn't even know he was doing it. In the language of his birth there was a phrase, "To swim in one's thoughts." He was nearly drowning in them.

The woman opened her mouth to speak, but changed her mind. "Nothing," she said.

The man in cell ten had taught him how to take the bread and pull it apart, wet the pieces, and shape them just so. With no window for sunlight, the pieces took two or three days to dry. The man taught him how to burn bits of paper—not fully, not until the ash went gray, but to stop it when the paper was black—then rub the ash into the bread. Soon he had a whole set: pawns, rooks, knights, bishops, a queen and a king.

The man told him to take off his shirt and turn it inside out and draw the board's squares there. And then, day after day, they would play. Queen to D-4. Bishop to B-3. "That's a bad move," he'd say. "I'll checkmate you in two moves." He was kind like that, but won nearly every game. While they played the man taught him philosophy. He started at the beginning, Aristotle, and went through to his favorite, Hegel. The boy recited poems—some of his, Lorca too, but mostly Hekmat, the Turkish poet.

He would say good night to the boy. Each night he would say it and then, "Try to count the stars."

And as the boy lay there in the dark he would feel excitement. Hope. Someday he would be out.

Cold air slapped his face. The girl was going out the door. She hadn't even said good-bye.

He looked at all the people in the café. All the space between them—it was as if each person was separated by the Great Wall of China.

Inches away, to his right, stood the café wall. He laid his hand on it. He felt for the roughness of the concrete, but it was wood and smooth. He leaned his ear toward it for a moment, then sat back. He missed that wall, the one through which for years someone had said, "Good night."

Lovely

The wind blows...
   ...and my love dances...within the breeze.
The flowers fill the greenhouse with their
excitement.

And I take cover behind the flower pots.

Thinking of the pine trees

In this frozen land
Where night rules sovereign
Life frozen in frostbite
And time frozen in wind chill

How green has it remained?

   How green?

Perhaps silence may be broken
   Perhaps winter may leave.
Perhaps there is hope.
   Perhaps the land is pregnant.
Perhaps there is spring
   A tomorrow

Someone said
   Forward?

Finger Tree

If sometimes you went to the city of Damascus
and you passed the neighborhood called Midan
(battlefield), you would find a tree there. The one
the children of the neighborhood call "Finger
Tree."

A Picture Above the Fireplace

I can see the rain out the window. The street lights are shining off the wet streets, and the smell of damp earth comes to me. It looks just the same as it did that night long ago, that night we talked until morning. I remember how the rain stopped just as the sun rose, and then she said, "Let's go out for a walk."

The street was full of cherry blossoms. We walked on them. Above us the sky was not angry anymore, but still heavy. We walked silently to the park. We found a bench there and sat down to feed a pigeon.

She took out a book from her purse and read a short story to me from Kawabata's book, *Palm-of-the-Hand Stories*, and afterward she picked up her Polaroid camera and took a picture of me and the pigeon. I closed my eyes; she was saying goodbye. I didn't want her to go. I wanted to be with her. When I opened my eyes again, I was inside her short story book, stuck with the pigeon between page 20 and 21.

I passed three springs there standing on those pages, reading the same lines over and over, talking with the pigeon. The pigeon told me about his family and the places he'd seen—

mountains, rivers, flowers, and I told him about my childhood and made up stories and wrote poems for him.

It was last winter when she came and picked up the book. The picture fell out, and she picked it up and looked at me. I wanted to talk to her but I couldn't open my mouth. I tried and tried, but I couldn't. She placed the picture on the bookshelf above the fireplace. The first night there, the pigeons flew away. I was by myself for a while until Van Gogh moved in across from me in the frame on the wall. We started to talk to each other in silence. From the other room we could hear Beethoven playing. We never saw him, but he was in there just the same. Van Gogh told me about his painting and his love—that he cut his ear off and gave it to her. When I asked him why, he said, "That's the only thing she wanted from me."

Last week Van Gogh moved upstairs to that room with the view of the farm, but still I hear him saying, "That's the only thing she wants from me." And the only thing she wanted from me was to quit smoking. I didn't do it. Now I'm by myself again.

The rain is stopping, the same as that morning. The sun is rising, and the street is full of cherry blossoms. I can hear her heart beat as she sleeps.

When she wakes up I will jump out of the picture and ask her to walk to the park. We will find the bench and sit together. I will take her hand and tell her I am sorry.

Tale and Table

I was thinking about you when Dianne arrived. I know she's still mad at me, I know I hurt her feelings. But she tried to deny it. She is kind and smart, and I'm sure I'd done something stupid again. Last week, we had a small argument about art. And later on in the movie theater when she waved her hand at me, I didn't go to her right away. I went to talk to David first. Then when I walked to her she was so cold.

Usually, she would stop to say hello on the way to class or home, but she stayed away for one week. Then she came to say goodbye before she left for Belgium.

I wanted to tell her I'm sorry. She kindly denied her anger, and left with a smile. But I didn't believe her smile.

I gazed at this table, and I don't know why the color of the table is green. I don't know what kind of wood it is. I wish I knew where it grew and who cut the tree. I don't know why this table is green.

Tom put down his espresso and gave me a hug. He sat with me. He did not let me ask him any questions. When I asked him how was his trip, he just said, fine.

He is a good friend of mine, but I haven't seen him for a year. All last year he was in France writing his book. You never met him, but I'm sure I've told you about him. He's very passionate, very sensitive: if the leaves fall from the tree, it makes him cry. He said, "There is going to be a war." He told me how he knows it's coming and I felt sad for him because when he lost his mother a couple years ago, he cried for days; now he thinks of all the mothers that will be lost in this war. I smoked a cigarette with him and then he left.

Hamid came and sat with me. He was sad because it was the 20th anniversary of an uncle's death. I asked him how his uncle died. Hamid said his uncle had just graduated from the university in the U.S., and came back to fight in the war.

"They came and told us he was dead," Hamid said, "but they couldn't find his body I was only six years old, and my mom and I went to where they brought the truck full of bodies. When they opened the truck door, blood ran out. We had to go through the bodies to try to find him. We couldn't recognize the faces. Sometimes it was just parts of bodies. It took us a whole month. Sometimes I would play with other kids there, and once I grew so tired I slept there among the bodies. My mom finally recognized my uncle by his socks, they were green, the ones he borrowed from my father the last time he was in our house."

Hamid left. These are the memories of when he was six, not being in a park and playing with his uncle or with children, but of death—no, no, I don't want to think about it. I want to run away from it. I want to think about something else. This table.

I don't know why the color of the table is green. I don't know what kind of wood it is. I wish I knew where it grew and who cut that tree. I don't know why this table is green.

I don't know why that man came and sat with me. I think he was around 60 years old. He picked up one of my cigarettes without asking, and began to complain about life. He complained about his nephew. He said his nephew doesn't listen to him. His nephew is 45 years old and lives in a shelter. His nephew doesn't know what life means.

He looked at one of the customers on the sofa in the corner. He says he likes women with big breasts. Twenty years ago when he was in Montana he slept in a whorehouse and a woman there had blonde hair and big breasts. Because of

that woman he stayed one week and every day
went to have sex with her. He told me her name,
but I forgot it.

He left and I didn't want to think about him
anymore. I remembered the first day of spring.
You came home with a bunch of white daisies.
You filled the blue vase with water and put the
flowers in it. We cooked dinner together, fish
and rice, of course with lots of garlic. Then you
put two candles on the table and lit them.

I never told you this, for you, the candles were
romantic, but they reminded me of the war, when
we didn't have electricity. For four years I
covered the window at night with cardboard and
could only read by candle. I read *War and Peace*
by candlelight. That night, I couldn't sleep
because war filled my mind.

That night I remembered my neighbor's son, Ali,
on the last day of the summer and watching him
fly his kite. A little while later a bomb dropped
on their house. The windows of my house were
destroyed and when I ran to theirs it didn't exist
anymore. I saw only smoke and dust.

Ali's sister was screaming over and over "I don't
want to die." She had a cut on her arm and I
bandaged it, telling her, "You're not going to die."
But then she pointed to Ali's arm laying in the

rubble and a piece of watermelon in the hand, and said, "What is this?"

I know you're going to come, but please don't bring a candle. Come and hold my hand, and read that poem for me, the one by Hekmet, the one that says "brother, bring me the book with a happy ending."

Last Day of the Summer

Inspired by Sohrab Sepehri

It was a summer afternoon,
the trees know which summer
Ruksanh was blowing life into a balloon
Ali was making a kite and
the radio in the corner of the room was on.
On the dining room table
  the watermelon watched the knife
Ali's mother lovingly prepared
  bread, cheese, and basil.

It was a summer afternoon
  attacks of sun on the earth
  attacks of shadows on the wall
the butterfly offends the red flower
an army of bees assault the grapes
the knife attacks the watermelon
the hands invade the plate.
War
  between teeth and bread
  attacks of warplanes on the child's kite
the balloon explodes

beneath the shattered fragments of the house
a piece of blood red watermelon
  beside Ali's hand.

I Want to Be a Butterfly

Just as yesterday, I want to write this story, but I don't know how to start. Probably I should start from long ago, when the guard came to my home and took my books, when they put bars in my window—the time when they stole the sun from the sky. Or maybe I should start from the night when that man told me to go home, the man who threw his lit cigarette at me, the night I was dancing with her. All through the dance I did not look at her, but she put her head on my shoulder and her hair smelled like chamomile flowers.

My grandma told me that in the old days a girl would give a strand of hair to a boy and tell him that if he ever needs her to just burn it and she will come. I smelled the chamomile. I wanted to touch her hair but I was scared. I wanted to steal a strand of it. Throughout the whole dance we did not talk. But I remember before the dance we had talked about colors and I told her that blue is the color of the sky, red the color of love, white the color of peace, yellow the color of hate, green the color of life. She laughed and I think she was green that night.

When she walked away I looked at the sky. I couldn't find my star. I thought that maybe my piece of the sky was lost—the piece my star was

on. I know it had a star. My father told me.
When I was a child I used to sleep under the sky.
I asked him why the sky is full of stars, and he
told me that everybody has a star. And when I
asked which one was mine he pointed to a small
red one. But I couldn't find it that night. I
thought that maybe I was dead. My mother said
that when you die your star will be gone. She told
me this when I couldn't see my grandma's star.
She said that people don't die, they just lose their
memory, that's all. They change into different
things, like flowers, birds, a tree. I think my
grandma became a pigeon because I saw a pigeon
that night sitting on the top of the tent, looking
at me kindly, as my grandma did.

No, I'm not dead. If I am dead, how can I
remember chamomile? I used to walk with my
grandmother across the prairie filled with plants
and flowers. She taught me which was good for
chest pain, which was good for a headache. She
told me to shut my eyes and smell the flower she
held under my nose. Can you name it? The last
time she asked me it was chamomile. I remember
the time, because I wanted to catch a butterfly.
She said no. I told her, I want to put it in my
book and keep it. She said, Butterflies are
beautiful when they fly. I told her that I want to
be a butterfly when I die. She said that I would
be a worm. I cried. She laughed and said some
worms can be butterflies, like a silk worm. I

remember. I haven't lost my memory.

I remember that night I walked home, just as the man at the bar told me to do when he threw his cigarette at me. I passed through the night until I came to the prairie. I couldn't see any of the tents. The tribe was gone to the other side of the mountains. The prairie was full of snow. It was too cold. And I came back with the wind and sat in this chair and gazed through the window at the people in the street. They passed as fast as the days of my life. A woman with her kids, a girl walking into the coffee shop, a man walking out of the shop with a cup of coffee. Kim walking her dog to the shop. Two students with backpacks walking from right to left, a student with a hat from left to right. The same as yesterday, the same as tomorrow. Weeks pass. A wall blocks my view to the other window. I wish it weren't there. That way I could see onto the street. I could see the bookstore.

I feel the silk winding around me. I may become a butterfly. If I do, I will fly around her hair. Or they may come and put me in hot water to kill me and harvest my silk. But if I become silk, I want to be blue silk. I would love to be a piece of thread in her clothes, close to her hair. I think I've sat in this chair too long.

Just as tomorrow, I will go to the bookstore. At

first I won't look at the books. I will look at the
people, at who buys which book. This woman
buys a book as a gift; she's more interested in the
cover. That man likes fiction. This girl with the
hat, she likes poetry. I see her all the time. I
think each of them is a book. I think if I saw her
again I should ask her, What's your title? I want
to read you.

Just as yesterday, I come back and sit in this chair
to write my story. It's the chair I always want to
write in, but I can't find my pen. I think I lost it.
No, I remember, the pen is there in the house, on
the empty bookshelf that holds my heart.

No, I'm not dead. I haven't lost my memory. I
remember when I fell in love. I remembered I
could dance to the beat of my own heart. I could
dance. But I wish I were dead. That way I could
be born again. I could lose my memory and I
could love again. My mother said that love is not
a shirt to change, that love is forever. She told me
that when my father died.

I remember when he went, he had a smile on his
face. Why can't I smile? Maybe I am wearing a
mask. But no, my hand tells me the truth. Maybe
I'm dead and I've become a bird. Birds can't
smile. Then I should find her and sing for her.
No, I can't fly. My mind can, but I can't. I know
how to walk. So I will walk into my memory.

I will walk up the mountain and down the other side past the river. The water will be cold. When I get to the prairie I will run and run until I come to the valley, then to the cave, the one I call Buried Alive. And I will see my father telling me that thousands of years ago, when the tribe had to go past the mountains, the way was so dangerous that they had to put the old people in the cave and leave food for them. When they came back in the spring, those still alive in the cave would rejoin them.

I will go and sit in the cave. And I will write my story, but I won't finish it there. I will wait for the tribe to come back in the spring. That will be a good time to finish. Spring, the green season. The season of creation. I want to have a good ending. I will wait until the rain begins to dance on the prairie and I will be a chamomile flower and she will pick me up and put me in her hair when the wind touches her breast. Or I will finish it when the sky becomes blue, when the children of our tribe make chamomile necklaces.

Seven Songs for Andrea

That's the end and I know it, but I don't know why. I think I will have to say good-bye to you soon. You should know that I wanted to write you that song. The one I promised you many years ago. But the stories won't let me. Anyplace I go they find me. When I catch the bus, they sit next to me. If I leave the bus and shop for groceries they bump into me in the aisles. At the coffee shop they are sitting there staring at me. I leave them at the table and, later, looking out the window, I see them walking in the street.

I don't want to think about them. I want to write a song. I don't know if Matt ever told you about the time we went to the Dinkytowner. We were sitting at a table when a man with two glasses of beer came and asked to sit with us. In the middle of all those people, he found me.

He said: "I had a girlfriend and I lived with her for five and a half years. I loved her and wanted her to be the mother of my children. I wanted to spend all of my life with her. But I have a mother who has Alzheimer's and a brother who is homeless and addicted to crack. My girlfriend could not understand why I helped them, or my love for them. She left me and went with someone else who had more money."

He disappeared between the customers. But later that night, I saw him again. He was on the ceiling of my bedroom when I was lying down. He was gazing at me. I closed my eyes. I didn't want to see him or think about him anymore, but he found a way to pass through my eye into my brain, and he said, "Write." He stayed there for a while and kept telling me to write. I didn't know what to do. I stayed at home and hid myself behind my books. After a while he finally left me alone, so I started walking on Nicollet Avenue.

I would often walk on Nicollet Avenue from 3rd Street to 12th Street, and then walk back. I did this almost every day. I know everybody's stand on Nicollet by heart. At nine and two o'clock, three men and two women come out for a smoke in front of the Excel Energy building. At ten and two a group of people come out for a smoke in front of City Center. There, a young homeless woman stands with her one-year-old child. On the same corner, another woman sells hotdogs out of a cart. Between 6th and 7th Streets is where the two homeless men sit and ask for change. In front of the IDS, there is young homeless woman with a broken leg who stands there. At Orchestra Hall Plaza a group sits sipping beer from paper bags. Once in a while I am stopped, and people ask for cigarettes or change.

This is what I did until last Thursday when I passed 12th Street. I did not come back. I just kept on going and going. I passed the entrance sign for Highway 35W South. Then I started to walk on the highway's southbound shoulder. I walked for a long time. After a while I realized that I was in the middle of the highway. The cars were honking their horns. I didn't look back. I didn't want to turn into salt, like the Bible says.

A police officer eventually stopped me. He was wearing sunglasses. I could not see his eyes, but he had a calm voice. He asked me where I was going. I told him, "To the other side of the world." The officer was silent for a moment and then asked me for my ID. He then called me by my name and asked me why I wanted to go to the other side of the world. I told him, "Wars, they want to destroy Civilization. There is no food, and people are dying. A lot of things are going on." He then asked me, "How do you know that there is no war on the other side of the world?" I told him "I know this because I saw it in my dreams."

All the houses on the other side of the world are blue with white windows and flowerbeds on windowsills. He then nodded his head and asked me why I didn't pack anything. I told him that over there people are kind and will give me what I need. He then asked me how I am going to get there. I told him that I would keep going straight until I reach mountains. Then I will turn right and keep going until I reach a river. I will then take a left and follow the river to the ocean. Then I will swim; when I get tired there will be a lot of boats to rest in. When I pass the ocean I will reach the other side of the world.

Then, the first thing that I will do is go to the park next to the library, and I will find that peach tree with flowers all around it. I will sit there. The officer stopped me. He pulled out a note pad from his shirt pocket and started to write something. I think he was writing down the directions. Before he could ask me any more questions, I told him that he should come with me. He said that it would be nice but today he has work to do, perhaps another day. But he could give me a ride for some of the way and introduce me to a person who knows a shortcut. I accepted, even though I had my doubts. While riding in his car I did not look back and didn't say anything. He didn't ask any more questions.

We drove for a while then stopped in front of a building. He said, "In that building is the person who will be able to help you." We walked in and inside a big white room he introduced me to an old woman with gray hair. Before taking off, he told her of my plan to go to the other side of the world. I stayed with her for a while; she offered me something to drink. I told her, "Water would be nice." She brought a glass of water then took me to another room. There was a man who introduced himself as Dr. Mike Anderson but he looked more like John McEnroe, the tennis player.

He asked me a lot of strange questions, like whether I was in trouble. Was I angry or depressed. Sad, perhaps? He asked me if I want to kill myself. I told him, "Of course not. Life on the other side of the world is beautiful." I remember him asking me if I slept well. I told him, "No." For a long time I have had a dream where I wanted to water the garden but I couldn't find any water. In the dream, I start to dig a well, but what I find instead is always mud and worms. Last night I had a different dream. I was on the other side of the world. I was sitting under a peach tree, surrounded by flowers, writing a song.

The doctor looked in his drawer, found some pictures and showed them to me. He asked me what I saw in the pictures. He wrote something on a piece of paper. He stood up and told me that I should rest here for a while. He promised to show me the shortcut later. He asked me to wait for the nurse in the next room. I sat there until the same gray-haired old woman came in and took me to "Ward 6."

For a moment I stopped and got excited. I told her Chekhov should be here. She said, "Who?" I told her Anton Chekhov should be there working on his play about that strange doctor. She said, "I don't know him." I told her to please go and check. He should be here. She went to her office and called someone. She then came back and told me, "He is on vacation and he will be back in a couple of days." Then she asked me, "Why do you want to see him?" I told her, "He is a very smart surgeon. He knows how to dissect society with his pen. I am very excited to see him and ask him if there is any hope."

She took me to a room and said I would be sharing the room with Mohammed. But Mohammed would not look at me or talk to me. His face was lined with worry, and his jaw was clenched. At first I thought he might be mute, but later on I realized he couldn't be mute because he was muttering to himself. I looked at him and said, "When Chekhov comes I will have someone to talk to."

The next morning John McEnroe showed up. Mohammed was under the bed and crying. I don't know why the doctor was pretending that Mohammed was not there. He wanted to know how I was doing. Did I have any plans for my days? I told him I didn't know yet. Right at that moment we heard music coming from the next room. McEnroe stopped and thought for a moment. Then he said, "Now is a good time to write your songs." I agreed. I didn't want to argue with him in case he would kick me out and I would miss my chance to meet Chekhov.

After McEnroe left I thought about you, Andrea. I remembered your sadness after your recent breakup. I thought, if I can write that song, you might be happy. I told myself I should write seven songs, not just one, but one for each day of the week. Then she could be happy every day. Yeah, that's what I will do.

A few days passed and Chekhov didn't come. For a few hours every morning I started writing the songs.

The rest of my time was spent in the TV room with Aaron the Doctor and Mr. Z, as well as John and Osman. Aaron, the Doctor thought marijuana was the solution for everything. Mr. Z was the African American guy who worshipped Malcolm X. He didn't like to play chess because he didn't like the racist rule: white always moves first. John was the one with a Bible in his hand; for some reason he was known as Mr. Shut Up. No one told me why. Osman was called The Paranoid. He didn't like to play chess because he didn't like that everybody could be killed just to protect a king. One day after lunch they told me that every Friday Mohammed hides under the bed. But they didn't know why.

On Thursday morning the nurse allowed me to use the phone, and I called my friends Liz, Nikki, and Chris. Chris did not answer the phone, Nikki was out of town. But that afternoon Liz visited me. Liz and I sat on the bench and started to talk. We remembered those star-filled nights of camping in Cook County. We talked of canoeing and harvesting wild rice. We talked for a while, and then she apologized because she had to leave. Liz had plans to go hiking and needed to pack. Before she left she gave me a pack of cigarettes that I had asked for. She said, "These are not good for you."

That evening I found a place to smoke. When I returned, Mohammed spoke to me for the first time. He asked me if I had a cigarette. He asked me if he could come with me the next time I went to smoke. I told him we could go after dinner. At dinnertime I think he didn't eat at all. He was waiting for me to finish. Later we went out to smoke.

He took a drag of the cigarette, looked into my eyes and said, "When I was nine years old, watching the pigeons on the roof of our house I saw my mother making love to a man. I didn't know what to do. I waited for my dad to come home. That afternoon I told him what I saw. He grabbed my hand and took me to my uncle's house, my mom's brother. My father asked me to tell my uncle what I saw. I told him what I told my father. My uncle didn't say anything; he went to the kitchen and came back. My father, uncle and I walked back to our house. He called my mother to the backyard, and in front of all of us, he slit her throat." Mohammed took a deep breath and continued. "Every Friday, my father would wake me up early in the morning and take me to prison to visit my uncle." Mohammed then took the last drag of his cigarette and walked away.

I stayed there for a while. When I walked back to the room I saw Mohammed sleeping for the first time.

I am now lying down on the bed and gazing at the ceiling. The sun arrives and throws Friday on the wall. I see Mohammed as a young boy holding his father's hand and leaving the room. Andrea, I can't finish these songs.

Sibel

If Mustafa's mom had had a few cents more,
Mustafa would have a sister

The Story of My Stories

People leave their homelands as refugees to save their lives, or to make a better future for their kids, or to get a few more bites of food. Many people are not lucky enough to even become refugees and never make it past their own country's border. They get arrested, or they step on a mine. Some people live in camps for years, others drown in rivers, or they pack themselves in containers and suffocate, or their ship sinks. The Cuban poet Elena Caruso says the mass of water between Florida and Cuba needs its own big cross.

But when you arrive as a refugee in your new country, different problems begin—problems of language, problems of culture. People look at you as an adult, but you are not an adult. You have to be born again. You have to learn the new language and the new culture. You have to learn to walk on snow.

Based on this, I decided to interview a lot of immigrants, on why and how they left their countries. My project was called *You Have to Learn to Walk on Snow*. But after getting started, my friend Brian's computer that held those stories crashed and the stories were lost.

Then came another idea, a new project: a book called *Walking in Kafka's Shoes*. The idea was to see myself as a young boy and *not* let that boy become me. As I wrote, I argued with that boy all the time. I told him, "Hey, those things you're doing, I've already done them and the result was this..." He tried to defend himself and to explain to me why he was doing them. I wanted to show the reasons for how I ended up in a different country. I carried this idea every day with me to work, and brought it back home, and at night tried to write it down. But almost every night, I threw my work in the garbage.

I remember one of those nights, my Mom called me. After talking with her, I lay down on the bed and thought about my house on the other side of the night. I thought about my friend Hassan. When he was executed his mother came to his killers and asked for his body, but they made her pay for the costs of his execution before they allowed her to claim his body. That night I didn't sleep. By the morning, before work, the idea of "The House of the Other Side of the Night," was born in my mind.

I was away for a while, living in Japan. When I came back I stayed at my sister's house. The first evening I remember my nephew was playing a computer game. In the game he was in a war and the more people he killed, the more money he got.

The next morning, I was reading an article about Afghanistan in the paper when my nephew complained there is nothing to eat.

My sister lives in one of those seven-bathroom homes. I'd already eaten breakfast and seen that she had a lot of different kinds of cheeses, cereals, jams.

When I asked about what he means I realized he is upset there were not white bread.

I looked through the cupboards and he was right: there were several different kinds of bread, but no white.

I sat back down at the table, and the first thing that came to mind was the people in Afghanistan, the kids. Then I thought about Baraki whom I'd interviewed for my first project. He ate meat only two times a year, and these were at religious celebrations. He told me that when he was a small boy, he had to walk four miles one way to school. High school was six miles each way. In the summertime, they made a ball of old clothes to play with. I remembered that story from my first project, and back then I called it "My First Pair of

Shoes." Baraki bought his first pair of shoes when he went to college.

I remember some of my own classmates when I went to school. A few of them had a pencil sewn into their clothes. Their families could not afford the risk of losing it and having to purchase another pencil.

My brain became pregnant with all these things for days, weeks, months. They became the inspiration for my story "Follow the Rain."

When I was in tenth grade, I used to study theater after school at a nonprofit organization. My teacher was a beautiful woman who became a kind of mother and friend of mine. Once, she took me to an eight-millimeter film festival. Afterward, she asked me if I liked it. I said No. She challenged me: "Can you make a better film?" I was young and proud and probably told her yes.

A few weeks later I wanted to make a film. She gave me her husband's equipment and money to buy film. I made a couple of short films and showed them in the next festival. Somehow they won first and second prizes.

During the school holiday, I traveled back to my hometown. It belonged to my tribe and was full of natural oil and gas. An oil company took the oil and burned the gas a few hundred yards away. But at the same time, some people in my tribe were so poor that they used dried cow shit for cooking.

I wanted to make a documentary to show how people of my tribe lived in poverty, with all the wealth that surrounded them. I was arrested with my friend Mohsen. They threw us into two different cells. Eventually they let us go, but they kept all the film and equipment, and they threw us out of the city with no money. That was when I said goodbye to filmmaking.

A while ago, I saw a movie by the person who used to make eight-millimeter films with me. Now he's a famous filmmaker. I thought about my own relationship with filmmaking. That's when I started to write "Story for Sale."

I love to read, but not too many books get me excited. I don't know why, maybe because I'm getting old. But when I read the speech that Octavio Paz gave at the Frankfurt Book Fair in the '80s—in which he described the sickness of literature today and how most bestsellers are junk; how publishers should say no to the writers, and how the writers should do as was done in the Renaissance when people began to write against the church—this was exactly my own thinking. Literature is now very close to bankruptcy.

I believe literature has a very difficult challenge today with time and technology. People are so busy now, they have almost no time. But so many writers take a lot of time and space and say nothing. They don't know the true life of their own characters. I started thinking of this idea of bankruptcy. At that time in the culture, the phrase Chapter Seven meant exactly that— bankruptcy. This is how the idea for the story "Chapter Seven" came to my mind.

One spring while I was walking down the street, I saw a pregnant woman working in her garden. She reminded me of my neighbor at home during the war. Back then I lived close to the airport. A lot of times, when they tried to bomb the airport, they missed their targets and dropped bombs in my neighborhood. Almost all of the families, who could, left town. But I had a neighbor who didn't want to leave. For her, life went on and she always spent her time in the garden planting herbs and flowers, taking care to make it so beautiful. I remembered how people tried to help each other; how they gave gas to others so they could leave town; or how they found food for older people—all those things came back to my mind. I could see them exactly as if it were in a picture. I wrote "Spring Comes through the South Window" hoping someday to turn it into a screenplay. So far that day hasn't come.

One winter day I took Aristotle's book *Politics* to the café. I'm lucky that I've met a lot of beautiful people, but that day I felt very lonely. I was writing poems on napkins when a woman came and sat with me. When she left, I looked at the crowd and thought, why do we have so many wars? What's happened with human beings? In *Politics,* Aristotle talked about the Persian Empire and how it didn't allow people to eat together or sleep together in the dormitories because they would have time to learn from each other. That was true. In third-world countries, it's still true. In third-world countries they put us in jail not because they don't like us, but because they don't like the way we think. They shoot us because they don't want our ideas to grow.

I remember Cervantes in *Don Quixote* said, "Human life was so beautiful, but all the problems in the world started when we began to learn the words 'mine' and 'yours'." I thought: We divide ourselves and make our own prisons. We carry our own walls: *this is my business and this is your business*; *this is my problem, and that's yours*. I looked at the crowd again and in my imagination saw the Great Wall of China. When I left the café, I brought with me the idea for "Behind the Wall."

One of the most beautiful people I've met is my friend Mazen. We get together sometimes. One night we were sitting and talking and he told me that when he was young, he wanted to go to America and be a pilot. Because of that, he started working at his father's tile factory to save money. He worked every day in summertime, and when school began, he went after he finished his homework. One night he got very tired. He fell asleep and the machine cut off his little finger and it fell in the grout they used for the tiles. By the time they found it, it was too late to stitch together. I started to write a story about it in my mind. I came up with the idea how he and his friends the next day on the way to school buried his finger under a tree. I called that story "Finger Tree". This is one of the many stories I buried in my mind.

One night when I was in Japan, I argued with my girlfriend who complained about my smoking. We argued all night. I was so stubborn in defending myself.

"You know I smoke," I said. "When you met me I was a smoker." I said this over and over again and refused to back down.

Kawabata has a short story collection called *Palm of the Hand Stories*. The stories were written between 1928 and 1972, the year he committed suicide. I love that book. He can say something so beautiful in only a page or two, never taking too much time or space. Years after our argument, I picked up that book and a picture fell out. It was a picture that my girlfriend had taken the day after our argument. I wanted to apologize to her. I used Kawabata's experience and wrote a page-long story, the one called "A Picture above the Fireplace."

It was one of those days when I was sitting at the green table in the coffee shop. It was quiet, not too many customers. First my friend Dianne came and sat with me. Then Tom came and we had coffee and talked, and after that Hamid came. When he left, a stranger came and we talked. After all of them had left, my brain became pregnant with these conversations. I wanted to bring them all together. I wanted to talk about Hamid's life, to let people know how he spent some of his childhood, what he carried. The result was "Tale and Table."

One night one of my friends invited me to go the club with her and dance. I don't know how to dance, but I tried anyway. Her hair smelled of chamomile. It reminded me of when I was a child, when my tribe used to migrate in the summer with the sheep and goats to find grass. My grandmother used to give me chamomile for my chest pain and she tried to teach me all the different plants and herbs. I live my life in two different worlds: my life with my tribe, and my life today. Coming back from the club that night, I couldn't sleep. Those two worlds occupied my mind. Every night for three weeks I'd wake in anxiety and think about those worlds. When I'd sleep, I'd dream about this: my grandmother was in my mind all the time, day and night, and wouldn't let my hand go; my mom too. After nearly three weeks, I finished the piece I called "I Want to Be a Butterfly."

Matt and I went to drink a beer, but Andrea didn't want to come with us. I gave her one of my stories, "Tale and Table," to read when I was gone. In the bar, we met a guy who complained about his life and then disappeared into the crowd. Matt and I had a couple more beers before we went back to the coffee shop. The first thing that Andrea said when we got back was: "How come you didn't talk about me in the stories?"

Andrea is very kind and has a beautiful voice, but she doesn't like my type of literature. I told her, "Andrea, I'm going to write a song for you." I've never written a song before—poems, yes, but no songs. I came back that night and started thinking about writing a song. But the guy I'd met in the bar wouldn't let me go. He was sitting in my bedroom with two glasses of beer in his hand and saying, "I had a girlfriend I loved, and I wanted her to be the mother of my children. But I have a mother who has Alzheimer's and a drug-

addicted brother, and my girlfriend couldn't
understand my help to them. She left me for
another guy who had more." Based on that talk, I
wrote the story "Seven Songs for Andrea," and I
left it there for years.

When I lost my job I didn't know what I should
do with my day. I woke up every morning and
walked on Nicollet Avenue from Third Street to
Eleventh Street and came back. On one of those
days I met my friend Osman on the street. I told
him I was just walking, and he laughed and said,
"Do you want to go to the end of the world?"

"What do you mean?"

He told me about the first Bush war, when he was
scared that Bush would kill him; so he started to
walk down the highway. He walked and walked
until the police came and took him to the mental
hospital.

That day after my own walk, I looked all over my
apartment for matches. I found the old story for
Andrea, the one I'd written years earlier. I read it
again, and, that night, the guy was back on my
ceiling. And I saw Osman too, walking in the
middle of the highway, blocking the highway,
cars behind him. I saw Mohammed, the one
Osman met in the mental hospital. The next
morning, after breakfast when I went for my

morning walk on Nicollet Mall, I carried in my mind a new version of "Seven Songs for Andrea."

I had dinner with my friend Mustafa, and told him, "Because I lost some of my hearing in the war, I can't recognize some sounds. For example, before I saw the words in writing I didn't know if the word was *kindergarten* or *tindergarten*; whether it was *vacuum cleaner* or *baccum cleaner*."

I asked Mustafa to write down his daughter's name. I wanted to see it so I could pronounce it. He wrote: "Sibel" and he said that was also his sister's name. I've known Mustafa for a long time, and I didn't know he had a sister.

He said, "When she was 6 months old, she died."

He continued: "When my sister was born, I was a couple years old. I was sent to my grandparents to live because we were so poor. One day Sibel got sick and my Mom tried everything to make her better. She didn't get better. She had a high fever. My Mom took her and ran through the street to get to the hospital. She didn't have enough money for a taxi, so she waited for the minibus to come. (Some cities have minibuses that go from one area to another the same as a taxi, though because they stop so often, the minibuses are much cheaper.) My mom begged the bus driver, 'Please, my daughter is dying, take me to the hospital.' But the driver kept stopping, dropping off and picking up passengers as usual. By the time Mom got to the hospital, Sibel passed away."

Tears came to my eyes, and I told him that's a beautiful subject for a story.

Mustafa said, "But it's sad."

I said, "I believe that to create happiness, you have to talk about sadness. To create beauty, you have to talk about ugliness. By saying these things, you ask people for help. People find a solution, and they create beauty, and they create happiness."

Mustafa agreed with me. But he also said, "Maybe situations like that happened all the time to the bus driver and he could not do that all the time." I agreed. Maybe the passengers didn't want to miss the stop because they'd be late and lose their jobs.

Now I carry Sibel in my mind. I think that if Mustafa's mom had had a few cents more, Mustafa would have a sister.